Falling Asleep/

Falling Asleep/

Falling Asleep/

A DreadLore Tale

by Bill Bunkum

DARKEYES PUBLISHING
Lexington, Kentucky

To our health: mental, physical,
and spiritual

Thanks to
Natalia Cline

~ and ~

The "Dreadies" DreadLore community

TABLE\ OF\ CONTENTS/

PROLOGUE/

chapter_1.1_AWAKEN\ ME/

chapter_1.2_METRO\ LINE\ BLUE/

chapter_1.3_RECOGNITION/

chapter_1.4_OUTBOUND/

EPILOGUE/_

Falling Asleep/

daria~$ cd PROLOGUE/

The year is unimportant, but while technology has advanced in *The Natural*, 'Zens still wrestle with themselves and the decisions others make...We are born lost in this fading light of a long fading star. We each find our way the best we can.

When no thing matters, the only things that could matter are those that we choose. Things which we choose to matter do so ultimately; they do so without reservation; they do so without hesitation; they do so without compromise, and with no strings attached.

Falling Asleep/

```
daria~$ cd chapter_1.1_AWAKEN\ ME/
```

An analog hiss proceeds his voice:

> *"I watch all I can of the setting Sun before getting bored and then walk inside the house. I don't know if it's really boredom or anxiety, but there's a nervousness I feel most of the time; it wards me away from continuing romantic endeavors. I'm just feeling so far away from you..."*

The voice pauses long enough for Daria to sigh and reach for her cup of tea. She rests her cigarette on the saucer and braces the cup with both hands to warm them. A scooting sound emits from the device and then the sound of the boy taking a careful drink of something hot. Daria snorts at the coincidence.

> *"The thought of losing time prevails – the task with which I currently invest myself isn't worthy enough of my full effort.*
>
> *"More random, marginal tasks usually win out. I find myself lying about in silence...angered when interrupted; my mind constantly wanders and seeks out some new stimulus. But, in this age of over-stimulus, it somehow finds no respite."*

Daria stops the relic, which halts with a loud chunk, and rubs the dryness from her eyes. She rocks herself to sit up and stretches like an eagle spreading its wings, then a ginger bend at the waist so

```
daria~$ cd chapter_1.1_AWAKEN\ ME/
```

her elbows rest on to her knees; her back hurts from lying still for so long on her stomach. Contorted and motionless, she lets her head hang to the side in an effort to loosen her ailing shoulder while her reverie continues like a flood, with closed eyes, as thoughts rush through the blackness of her mind.

All is interrupted when a grumble in her stomach alerts her of how long she has laid in bed fencing with sleep. She had not noticed the sick, morning light starting to creep beneath her heavy curtains clinging over the bedroom windows. She groans at the blue light reflecting off of the wooden floor and into her eyes. Turning over, she wraps the bed sheet around her like a toga and lays on her back to stare and blink at the ceiling of her solitary apartment.

The glass in the window shakes as a craft thrums near. Daria sighs heavy and along with the craft's humming. She sneaks out from under the sheet, climbing off the bed, and tenses when the pads of her feet touch the floor. Her knee knocks the palm-sized relic rattling across the floor in the process. "**Ah, shit!**"

Daria slumps to pick it up and is surprised to not feel her hair fall over her ears and eyes. She chews her lip. She remembers having it cut yesterday, all of it, and then she donated it – all of it. The boy on the recording always liked her long hair. She huffs and reminds herself that her donation was not a half-hearted attempt to justify the act. She likes the convenience of her bob, no lengths of black hair clogging the shower, no need to style or comb it, none of which the boy would accept. She struggled with her decision for over a week before heading to the salon – even there she thought about how disappointed he would be seeing those tresses litter the floor. Standing straight up with a bounce, she glares at the relic and imagines it glaring back at her as he would. As if the relic's casing were a yellow eyeball which the floor's had somehow manifested.

The eyeball gazes dumb and unblinking at her. Daria conquers the urge to cry as she stands alone wearing nothing but the flimsy shirt from this past lover and those same plain-Jane panties. A low beep from beneath the turmoil of her bed reminds her to check the time; she mines her phone from the covers and turns it over. Blocky letters flash her the phone's complaint. **"Again? Craster, I gotta get to work."**

Daria tosses the relic again into the pile of covers. She lumbers into the tiny bathroom, her motion triggering an amber light to flicker on. She pulls off the dingy shirt, flips on the shower, and with a bump and a slam, uses her heel to shut the bathroom door behind her.

```
daria~$ cd chapter_1.1_AWAKEN\ ME/
```

```
daria~$ cd chapter_1.2_METRO\ LINE\ BLUE/
```

The metro car whips around the corner in arc so smooth most of its inhabitants fail to notice. Oscillations in the rushing wind as it buffets against the car's glass clue a body in that they're even moving – that and the rushing by of buildings and college trees as they pass another campus. The car auto-senses a tunnel's approach and switches the in-cab lighting with such seamless precision that even Daria is impressed.

Little can be done about the echo. The car's speed breaks through the air with such force that it rebounds off nearby structures back and forth to resonate. Tunnels are the worst. The harmonic seems to last forever, an endless dance that grows in intensity from end to end.

Fear that the car could derail stabs her in the gut like bad cramps. She breathes in deep one and reminds herself that the thought is irrational. Breathing does nothing for the pain; then the sweats come. She jerks her head up from gazing into her lap and scans the other passengers' faces to see if the fear is mutual. Opposite her sits a man with ebony skin wearing his toboggan pulled down so low that it nearly covers his eyes; a smile plays on his lips as he hums something

```
Falling Asleep/
```

melodious but not loud enough to make out over the car's echo. Beside the man sits an elderly woman. She is knitting a scarf with more colors than Daria knows what to do with. At the end of the car, several students wearing their winter clothes, their backpacks shouldered and layered with their school's patches, chatter on in an endless garble.

Daria nestles back into her seat, not surprised everyone is oblivious, into the comfort of the sable folds of her coat. She returns her gaze to her lap and then to her handbag, its leather darkened and wrinkled with time – it had been her grandmother's once. The thought somehow calms her.

"When did I become such a *pussy* about this stuff?" she mutters.

The echo dies down and the metro lights flicker off as the car climbs and exits the tunnel. Dim lights switch on better marking the aisles and a human-sounding voice emits from unseen speakers.

"Please, fasten your seatbelts and stay in your seats. The weather is fairer than expected, so the train is speeding up."

"Ah, fock."

The man humming smiles at her.

"You'll be fine," he reassures her.

Daria attempts to smile back but instead snorts. Magnetic repulsors kick on and the car jolts from side to side taking flight, now hovering meters above its tracks. Passengers instinctively grasp their belongings tighter and brace themselves as the car accelerates. What

```
daria~$ cd chapter_1.2_METRO\ LINE\ BLUE/
```

was a grey, industrial city outside the car windows transitions into a mottled blur of concrete high rises and streaking lights.

"**On**," she commands and the earbuds she perpetually wears blink to life.

The train soars through the air. Daria closes the blinds next to her and waits for the relic to start playing. After a moment, she remembers it's unequipped to receive voice commands. With a huff, she fumbles in her handbag for it and presses **Play**.

"...and, I was 30,000 feet high when I realized it. As an aside, the thought came to me that I was so high that the clouds were <u>low</u>. That is something, don't you think?"

Someone on the recording chuckles, a voice other than the boy's but similar and at a distance, as if the speaker had been sitting across from boy. Daria notes the timbre as that of an older man.

She presses **Pause/Stop** and thinks, *"**His dead father?**"*

The boy had only talked about his father on a handful of occasions. Daria was tempted by the notion that the boy would allow himself to have a role-model, and she would press him every so often for elaboration. The boy would either brush her off with a simple joke, or he would spin a yarn about something his father had once said, or done, and then drop a punchline that shook anyone in the room with fits of laughter.

Conversation on the topic ended altogether after his father died. Daria had to draw the cause of death out of the boy like a doctor would poison – cancer. She never knew which kind. She hadn't even known the boy's father had fallen ill.

It was impossible now, of course, but she would love to meet the man. Daria imagines the two of them having a good conversation about how his son treated her those last few months, or better yet, that last year.

"People should not just up and leave the person they are supposed to be in love with," she thinks.

She furrows her eyebrows and imagines her ex's response.

"You didn't owe me anything," she murmurs, **"but you were supposed to love me."**

She is suddenly aware that she is talking to herself in public (again). She folds her legs up into the chair and hides in the furls of her coat like a spy looking left and right to see if any of the other passengers are eyeballing her. No one is paying attention to anything but themselves: his phone, her book, her scarf; that one stares with as much character as "Stop" sign at the floor – Daria frowns.

She struggles within her black gloves for the `Play` button.

"She was looking at me from acrost the cabin, a Chinese girl. No, I wasn't attracted, but she had these eyes that made me think."

"Yeah, think about what?" the older man asks.

```
daria~$ cd chapter_1.2_METRO\ LINE\ BLUE/
```

"I guess there was something tired about her eyes, like she'd been thinking. She kept on looking over at me whenever I looked at her."

"You were creeping her out – making her feel silly."

"I'm dunno. I think she was just nervous to be on the plane, maybe a first-time-flyer? I dunno. But, seeing her there, lounging in that big, green coat, like a Hunter green, and conversing in Chinese with, I guess it was her friend, about God knows what…"

"Maybe she thought you could understand her."

"I mean, I could, but I wasn't listening."

Daria snarls. **"You always were a fockin'…pig fockin' bastard!"**

Her eyes wander mid-snarl back towards the elderly woman who now stares at her with bulbous, critical eyes. Daria feels the heat of a blush creeping into her cheeks. Just as quickly, annoyance strikes.

"**Sorry**," she heaves with as much grace as a drunk curtsey and rolls her eyes so far back into her head that it hurts.

She does not see it but the elderly woman frowns like a judge at her display; the ebony skinned man sends Daria a toothy smile, and chuckles, "You tell 'em, girl."

Daria locks daggers for eyes at the man – he finds somewhere else to look.

Falling Asleep/

```
daria~$ cd chapter_1.2_METRO\ LINE\ BLUE/
```

daria~# sudo cd chapter_1.3_RECOGNITION/

Daria smokes on the stoop outside of her apartment. The stoop doubles as the last step of several flights of concrete stairs which hug the four walls. They wind their way all the way up from the bottom ending at the top floor and then Daria's apartment door. Her apartment isn't technically on a floor of the building, more like an after-thought to the roof, and built sometime after the building was finished. Daria doesn't know the truth of it, nor does she care.

She looks down the square-shaped hole of the stairwell, all the way to the bottom where the apartment building's big, ornate door stands sentry against the riffraff. The boy had made fun of that door too many times to count saying that it "didn't match the drapes."

Daria never understood what he had meant but figured some mundane, sexual innuendo was involved. **"He was usually talking out of his ass,"** she mutters.

She takes a stunted draw from her cigarette and notices it's finished; patting her jacket pocket for another pack reassures her that she has more where that came from. She pushes **Play**.

Falling Asleep/

"Everything is distraction for me. Everything is —" A coffee pot gurgles in the background of the recording.

No judgment here.

"This thing never works right."

She hears the sound of the boy banging on the old pot with his fist. Daria had told him a hundred times that didn't work. ***It's just old. Old things take time.*** He would go ahead and do it anyway. She smiles to herself at the memory. She hears another couple bangs and then his sigh of exasperation.

"I mean, everything — it goes way beyond irritability. There's a word for it: irascibility. Do you know what that means?"

Laughter? No, not quite laughter. Daria's eyes widen. It's a girl's giggling and then her voice, *"No, not at all. What's it mean?"*

"Basically, it means I have a bad temper."

"But, you seem so calm…."

Daria pictures the face attached to that voice. She's cute.

"If I had one word to describe myself, it would be that singular word. Irascibility…you want a coff—"

Daria clamps down on the **Stop** button and white-knuckles the relic; she fights the urge to smash the thing. Turning on reflex, and craning her neck, she stares back at her apartment. **"Was that bitch in *our* kitchen?"** she growls.

A sour taste gathers into her mouth, and so without thinking, she gathers two cigarettes from the pack, one for her and one for… she glowers at the mistake. Daria shakes her head dropping the extra cigarette to the ground, stomps on it, and it feels good. Satisfied with

```
daria~# sudo cd chapter_1.3_RECOGNITION/
```

the mistake under her boot, she lights up hers and breathes in a portion of hell – she lit the wrong end.

A herculean coughing fit ensues which she knows will result in her upchucking those instant noodles from lunch. In an effort to avoid spewing across her own porch, she jerks herself up to her knees, ripping her leggings on the concrete in the process. Too full of bile to curse, Daria lunges her head forward and hangs it over the edge of the railing just in time to see noodles rain out of her mouth. She hangs there like a knocked out fighter on the ropes heaving into the chasm, all the way down to the bottom. Splash!

Convinced she's finished at last, she stumbles away from the railing and seeks balance from the brick wall behind her. Sweat drips from everywhere stinging her now exposed, bloody knees.

Winter doesn't seem so cold to her now. She takes in gulps of the cool air until she catches her breath. She balls up the cigarette and chucks the ruined thing over the railing. Then, she returns to her spot, plopping down and snatching up the relic from where it fell. She mashes the **Fast-forward** button. After a few seconds of whirring tape, Daria presses **Play** but realizes her earbuds have turned off.

"**On**," she grumbles.

She feels the familiar buzz of her left earbud but nothing in her right. Fingering her ear like something injured it, Daria scoots around the stoop looking for the fallen earbud.

daria~# sudo cd chapter_1.3_RECOGNITION/

She looks around the dingy stoop but finds nothing. Sighing, she glances over the railing and peers into the stairwell. A tiny gleam from down below at the foot of the stairs reveals where the earbud fell while she vomited.

"Damnit."

Daria mopes her way down the stairwell, passing the elevator without so much as a glance, and descends the stairs to the end. She breathes a sigh of relief when she finds the wayward earbud missed her pool of vomit. Seeing the pool of ejected noodles up close, she marvels at how much content came out from her. The stuff is splattered everywhere, but most seems to have coated the floor in front of the only elevator. Daria snorts at the sight.

Snatching up the earbud, she wipes off the dirt, tries to blow out whatever might be lurking still, and replaces it firmly in her ear. Sensing its counterpart already engaged, the replaced earbud hums to life. Daria presses `Play` but quickly mashes `Fast-forward` again when she hears the same girl's voice.

"I looove ethnic music, too!" she coos.

After a couple of frustrating attempts to skim past the conversation, Daria ejects the tape and flips it, reinserts it and starts it playing again. A brief hiss and she hears fingers fumbling with the antique microphone he loved to use.

There's an inhale before the boy starts speaking.

"Anything you wanted to talk about?"

Falling Asleep/

"I just figured…"

Daria tenses when she hears her own voice.

"You're always using this old thing and recording your deep conclusions about everything. I thought it would be nice to record something about…us."

The boy chuckles.

"Okay then, I'll ask again, what do you want to talk about?"

"I guess, well, what do you think about love?"

"Uh, okay. Can you be more specific, please?"

"Uh, okay, do you think there's a difference between being 'in love' with someone and just 'loving' someone?"

Daria rolls her eyes and groans.

"Are you asking if I love you, Daria?"

"I mean, are you 'in love' with me?"

He laughs again. Daria continues groaning. She finds her way to the big, ornate door looking for both a figurative and literal exit.

"Of course, I love you…"

The protracted pause is matched with uncomfortable shifting – both her's and the boy's.

"But…?"

Before she can enter the exit code into the keypad, the door's lock clinks and the door swings open. Daria mashes the `Stop` button. A red-haired man enters the foyer carrying his groceries under one arm, no bags. It's the guy with the grand piano who lives on the second floor. She remembers him complaining to anyone who would listen about not landing a first floor apartment.

```
daria~# sudo cd chapter_1.3_RECOGNITION/
```

The pianist tries to catch Daria's eye as they pass one another but she looks the other way and slips out the door. As the door closes behind her, Daria hears him shouting. "Oh, come on! Who puked all over – it's on my shoes for fock's sake!"

Falling Asleep/

```
daria~# sudo cd chapter_1.3_RECOGNITION/
```

The light of day is fading. The surrounding buildings are dark towers against a pale sky, cutting out only a thin strip she can see. Daria sees orange-tipped clouds growing ever pink, then purple. She marvels at how quick the day has passed since she got home. Parked cars line the narrow street in front of her apartment – most people have already eaten dinner.

Daria descends the steps outside of the ornate door and plops herself onto the bottom step. She holds **Rewind** for a fraction of a second, then mashes the **Play** button again.

"...I love you..." the boy hesitates.

*"**But...?**"*

"But, we have been dating for over 2 years. How could I not be in love with you?"

*"**That's not the same thing, is it?**"*

"Okay, here we go again..."

Daria stops listening. She pulls her knees up and rests her chin on them as she watches the last bit of daylight fade. Nighttime descends, and after some time, she notices the blue reflection cast by her earbuds blinking out as they go into **Power-Save** mode. All at once, she stands up and shivers

Falling Asleep/

head to toe – a stark contrast to the stillness of the sleeping neighborhood. Rubbing her eyes in an effort to wake herself from the mind fog, she climbs the stairs back towards her apartment, but hesitates at the door.

Her hands search for something in her jacket pockets: keys, cigarettes, chapstick, pocket knife, but no yellow relic. She pats herself down again – nothing! Spinning around, Daria searches the landing to no avail. She strips off her jacket and turns out its pockets with all of her items clattering to the concrete landing in disarray.

"What the fock? How'd I –"

Daria spots it. The relic rests on the steps where she had been sitting, right where she'd left it. In a huff, she marches down the stairs and snatches it up.

The recording had stopped by itself; she remembers these relics did that sort of thing. The tape's finish line having been reached, it was now ready to turn over again. She cannot remember the last part she'd heard.

"I suppose that's the way of things." Her voice sounds foreign to her.

Cold air claws at the warmth of her breath and transforms the atmosphere of the landing into the severity of a bygone era. Daria had seen such in antique films, the ones that were her favorites. The fiction plays out in her mind as she imagines the color around her fading into the grey tones of a dark and stormy street. She sits the relic back where she found it and stares. She stares gravely at the

```
daria~# sudo cd chapter_1.4_OUTBOUND/
```

relic, as gravely as she can, positioning her body to emulate that of a femme fatale.

She continues the goofy pose, cranes her neck and gets into it, until she feels nostalgia surge upwards from her abdomen. The silliness of it all, a memory of laughter and good times, of making fun. She remembers the voice, and then she remembers the face; with a start, Daria breaks her fantasy. She bends down. She snatches the relic up again. She descends the stairs two and three at a time until the sidewalk and then the street.

Daria races to one of the neighborhood trash bins leaning against a lamppost. She no longer feels the cold. Throwing the lid open, she launches the relic into the darkness and the smell with a heave, a hoarse cry, and as much violence as she can muster. The clang and metallic echo rob her of the catharsis for which she had desired. She jumps back in surprise of the sound and jerks again when the metal lid slams shut.

Dumbstruck in the newborn silence, Daria stares at the bin with a memory of metal on metal ringing in her ears. She fights the urge to save the relic from its destruction and instead ruffles through emptied jacket pockets. A frantic search later, she discovers a single cigarette stashed in her back pocket. She straightens the mashed up thing with care, but then without a lighter, is unable to smoke it; the rain comes but she doesn't notice.

Falling Asleep/

A slow walk in the mounting rain, dream-like movement up the stairs, and Daria gathers her things strewn across the landing. She singles out the lighter, and crouched with the rain soaking her hair, she takes the time to light what's left of the cigarette – it smolders then lights. It's enough.

Practice allows her to thumb the passcode into the keypad of the big, ornate without thinking. The lock clinks, and the door swings open. Daria enters the empty lobby dripping water everywhere. She stops in the middle of the room standing in the center of the Arizaad mosaic that's fashioned into the floor.

Looking up, her gaze follows the long staircase hugging the walls all the way to her apartment door at the top floor. Her vision blurs as her eyes track the smoke curling upwards from her cigarette into the heights and emptiness of the stairwell. The wet cigarette fails. She takes a moment to consider the elevator.

"Fock that," she snorts.

Daria passes by the elevator and reaches the stairs without checking to see if her noodle-mess was cleaned up. She begins her ascent back to her apartment. Along the way, she encounters no one. The only sounds she perceives are her own breathing and the rain outside, both steady and methodical, and the occasional snore from beyond an apartment doorway. A few failed attempts at lighting soaked cigarettes later, she reaches the top floor. Eyes to the ground she notices a stomped cigarette – the one she'd thrown out earlier.

Daria pauses in her doorway. She finds her apartment as she'd left it. Her favorite lamp casts soft, amber light across the modest

```
daria~# sudo cd chapter_1.4_OUTBOUND/
```

living room. Her open journal, a meager dinner, and a pack of fresh smokes lies on the ground where she'd been floor-sitting next to her couch. She draws on the stomped cigarette hanging in her mouth and frowns at the still lit candles. One candle crackles on her work desk while the other burns away on the table in the connected kitchen area.

"Gotta stop doin' that," she half-sings to herself.

Daria steps over her work clothes which she'd tossed aside in a heap and gathers up the bag of uncooked veggies and crackers left derelict. As she makes her way to the bedroom, she blows out the candles and stows what's left of "dinner" in the fridge.

It's dark inside her own room. No light slithers its way beneath the curtains. The night feels heavy and complete. Daria slinks out of her clothes and down to her skivvies in one, well-practiced motion. She pads into the small bathroom, and in the darkness, towels off her damp hair and rinses off her face. Teeth brushed and bathroom used, she pads back into her room. One last puff and she snuffs out her cigarette onto the bare nightstand. Easing herself into bed, she lies back beneath thick, poofy covers.

With a smile, Daria falls asleep.

Falling Asleep/

```
daria~# sudo cd chapter_1.4_OUTBOUND/
```

daria~# sudo cd EPILOGUE/

The decisions others make is outside of my control. It's their responsibility, not mine. If there's a god, or gods, or powers that be, I think they understand that.

The time others spend worrying whether they're in the right or wrong cannot concern me. Right or wrong, we've all got to deal with the consequences.

If I've learned one thing in my time it's that there is only time. Right now is my only time - time to act, time to feel. Outside of this moment, there may be some thing - a time to be, a time to dream.

I'll cross that bridge when I get to it...and I'll be awake for it.

Falling Asleep/

daria~# sudo cd EPILOGUE/

Darkeyes Publishing

Falling Asleep/

Further Reading

Dive deeper into the DreadLore world of Craster with these works by Bill Bunkum:

- *DreadLore Corebook*: Available in hardback, paperback, and digital formats—your guide to immersive storytelling and gameplay.
- *The Dark*: A newsletter exploring the mysteries, stories, and lore of the DreadLore world.
- DreadLore materials: Enhance your adventures with guides, playbills, and more.
- Upcoming stories: More tales from Craster and beyond are in the works.

Follow Bill on social media for updates and exclusive content:
- Official: https://darkeyespublishing.com
- Tabletop RPG: https://dreadlore.com
- Twitter/IG: @dreadloresystem
- YouTube: https://www.youtube.com/@dreadloresystem
- All Else: https://darkeyesdesign.com

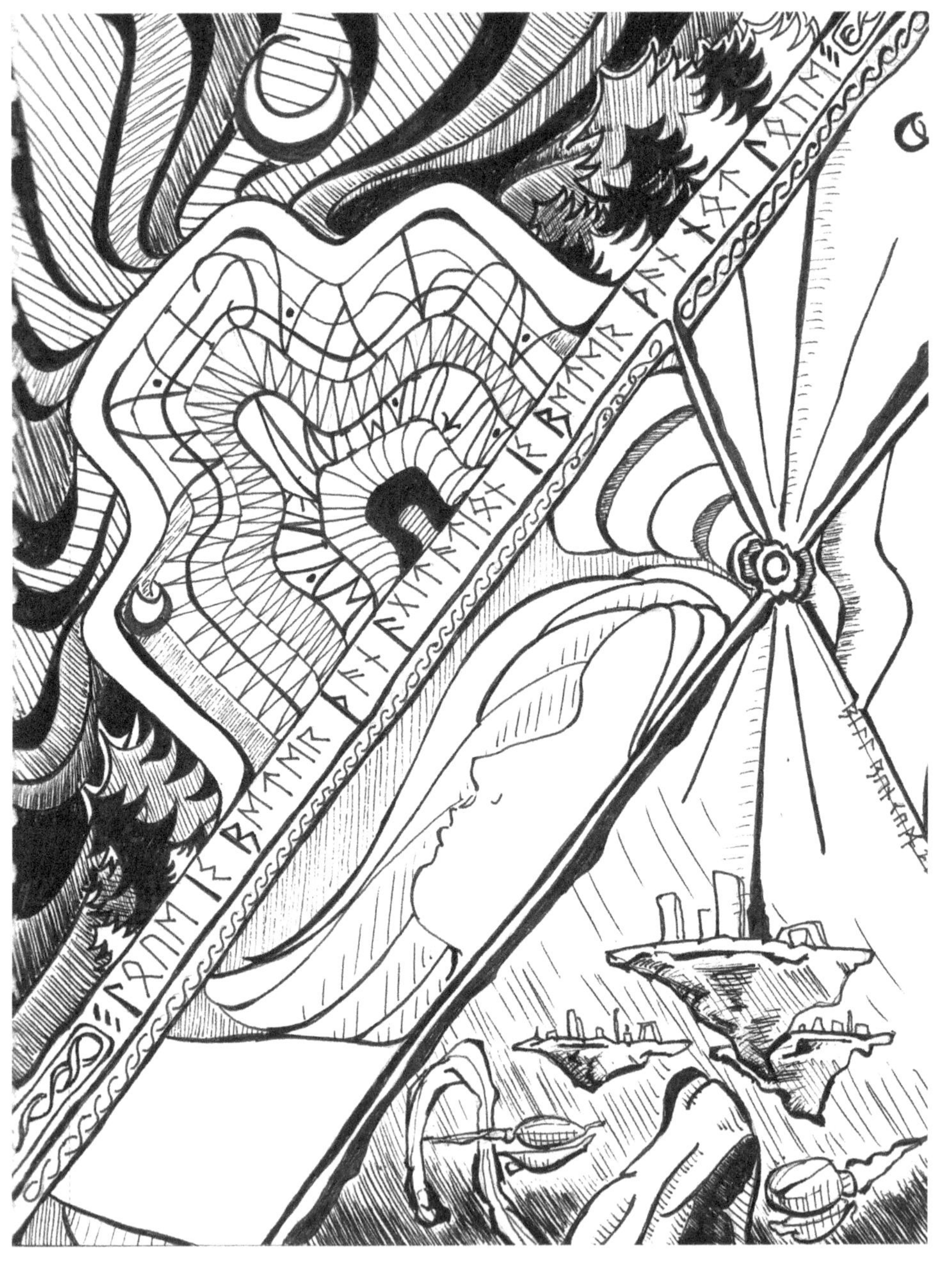

Falling Asleep/

ABOUT THE AUTHOR

BILL BUNKUM has been crafting stories and games for years, including the tabletop RPG *DreadLore*. A Kentucky native now based in Los Angeles, he writes tales set in the strange and sprawling world of Craster. When he's not at the keyboard, you'll find him shaking up cocktails for friends or pondering the next adventure.